CONTENTS

WHY ARE PLANTS SO GREAT?

What can be used to make string, to treat stomach ache, to clean wounds, contains vitamin C and calcium, can defend itself, is full of helpful insects that protect food crops helping farmers and gardeners, and grows all over the world? It's the humble stinging nettle. And this isn't the only plant with amazing abilities!

Plants are the foundation of all life on Earth – without them, we cannot survive! They provide food and medicine, clean the air we breathe, provide habitats for animals, protect against disasters, such as flooding, and are used to make products that we use every day.

The way that we use plants today can be linked back to our early ancestors. Plants were our first forms of fuel, shelter and food. Today, they are still used in everything from clothing to building, and most recently, as a way to reduce our use of plastics.

Our world is facing an environmental crisis. Global warming has caused climates around the world to change. This leads to natural disasters and the collapse of ecosystems. Pollution from industry and rubbish causes more problems for nature. While plants are threatened by these issues, they may also be the heroes who can save our planet! Let's find out how ...

CAN PLANTS REALLY SAVE THE WORLD?

WHAT ARE PLANTS?

Green moss growing on a roof, daisies in a park, cacti in a desert and giant redwood trees: plants range from tiny weeds to vast trees!

All organisms on Earth can be divided into groups by the characteristics they share. The plant kingdom contains nearly 400,000 species and more are being discovered all the time. Most plants have roots, stems and leaves. One thing that most plants have in common is photosynthesis.

Photosynthesis is an incredible process that plants use to make their own food. Plants contain a green pigment called chlorophyll. Using energy from sunlight along with chlorophyll, plants convert water and carbon dioxide into sugar and oxygen. The plant uses the sugar to grow. The oxygen is a waste product for the plant, and it releases it back into the air.

During the day, plants take in carbon dioxide and give out oxygen. As humans breathe, they give out carbon dioxide and take in oxygen.

We also produce carbon dioxide by burning fossil fuels for power. Too much carbon dioxide is harmful to the health of our planet. It traps the Sun's heat inside our atmosphere leading to global warming.

Plants provide the oxygen we need to breathe and take in carbon dioxide that harms our environment – what heroes!

WEB OF LIFE

The web of life shows how all living things rely on each other. All organisms need nutrients to live and grow. The web of life allows nutrients to be passed from plants to animals, and back to the earth again.

Plants are the first link in most food chains. As well as making food through photosynthesis (see pages 6-7), plants also take in mineral nutrients from the soil through their roots. When an animal eats a plant, it takes in the food and nutrients, using them to live and grow. When an animal eats another animal, the nutrient transfer continues. Without plants, the chain would break.

The web of life exists in all ecosystems around the world. It can be broken down into smaller food chains.

When plants and animals die, the nutrients in their bodies go back into the soil. New plants can then use these nutrients. This completes the cycle. Plants also contribute to the nutrient cycle as they drop their leaves and fruit which rot back into the ground.

TREMENDOUS TREES

Trees are the giants of the plant world! These enormous structures can reach over 100 m tall and live for thousands of years.

Wide branches provide shade and shelter. Their paper-thin leaves take in harmful gases from the air. This helps especially in cities where air pollution from vehicles and industry is higher. In cities, tree canopies help to control temperatures that can soar in hotter months.

Trees do an important job below the ground too. Their roots spread wide, branching into thinner and thinner strands. While they gather water and nutrients, roots also anchor the tree in the soil. The roots' paths make it easier for water to be absorbed into the ground, reducing the risk of flooding. In cities, tree roots help to filter and clean groundwater.

Wind and rain can wear away soil. This not only reduces the nutrients in the land for growing crops, but it means that waterways become clogged with soil and flooding increases. Trees provide a barrier between the weather and the land, and their roots hold soil in place.

Trees are one solution to the climate crisis. Many tree-planting initiatives have been set up but we must remember that trees take a long time to grow. We should protect existing older forests, as well as planting new ones.

HOME SWEET HOME

Owls peeping from hollow trees, birds building nests in trees, mice curled up in dry grasses: these are some of the first plant homes that we learn about. Ecosystems depend on animals, and animals depend on plants.

Providing animal homes benefits the plants too. Nesting birds help to control insect populations on and around trees.

Bees and wasps are important pollinating insects. Solitary bees nest in holes made in wood, soil or hollow plant stems. Paper wasps chew wood into a mash which they use like papier-mâché to sculpt their nests. Wasps nest near crops and eat the pests that damage them.

Orangutans spend their whole lives in trees, travelling from branch to branch and building leafy nests to sleep in. They eat more than 500 plant species and spread the seeds as they poo, replanting the forest. Sadly, orangutans are now seriously endangered because their forest habitat is being cleared for other uses.

Beavers cut down trees and shrubs to dam waterways, creating homes called lodges. The biggest lodges can reach 500 m wide. Beavers' dams help to create wetland habitats for other water plants and creatures to live in. They also divert and store water helping to control flooding, and their constructions trap sediment helping to clean water.

WORKING TOGETHER

Plants face many threats, and you might think they are helpless. But in fact, many plants have clever ways of defending themselves using warning signals.

If one plant is attacked by leaf-eating aphids, it releases a chemical from its leaves into the air. When the leaves of nearby plants take in these chemicals, they start making their own chemicals that repel aphids and attract aphid-eating predators, such as wasps.

Below the ground, thin strands of fungi grow through the soil and around most plants' roots. They exchange nutrients and water with these plants, but they also carry chemical messages between plants. Fungi extend the reach of most plants' roots, connecting plants together and creating a vast network. Plants can communicate across areas as huge as forests.

Plants use these systems to warn each other of drought. If one plant experiences a dry spell, it will send out a message. Other plants then close the stomata (tiny holes) on their leaves to avoid losing water.

Plants also recognise their own offspring. They allow these plants more room to grow than stranger plants, who they treat as competitors, and they can even pass them nutrients.

Our planet is changing. Plants that can defend themselves and work together will be key to protecting ecosystems and providing the world's food.

POLLUTION MONITORS

Buzz buzz, a hungry fly looking for some lunch settles on something bright red and fruity smelling. It's just getting ready to tuck in when ... SNAP! The plant closes around it. This is the Venus flytrap.

The Venus flytrap is a carnivorous plant. These plants have roots and leaves like other plants, but because they grow in poor, rocky ground, they have found another way to take in nutrients: eating insects.

Carnivorous plants have evolved to live in poor environments. Eating insects gives them nutrients that they cannot find in the soil. Studying carnivorous plants helps scientists to learn about the way that plants evolve and adapt over time.

In northern Europe, carnivorous sundew plants grow in boggy ground fed by rainwater. There is little nutrition here, so the sundews produce a sticky syrup that looks like drops of refreshing dew. But when an insect lands, it gets stuck and the plant draws it in. Yum.

However, some sundew plants have started making their leaves less sticky, so are catching fewer insects. This is a sign of air pollution.

As humans burn fossil fuels, nitrogen-rich pollutants are released. They mix with the air and return to the land with the rain. Sundews take in these substances and don't need to eat as many insects. As these plants behave differently depending on how close to pollution sources they are, they are helping scientists to find out more about how humans affect the planet.

WE NEED WEEDS

In April 1986, a nuclear reactor at the Chernobyl power plant in Ukraine exploded and spread radiation into the surrounding area. This area remains radioactive and no one can live there. But what can be seen are the plants that grow through apartment blocks, inside hotels and around schools, weaving between paving slabs and flowering on windowsills. Understanding plants' ability to regenerate an area is vital to restoring native habitats around the world.

Weeds have evolved to grow on bare ground, where they don't have competition from bigger plants. They produce lots of seeds to give themselves the best chance of success. Many produce seeds that can be carried by the wind, allowing them to spread easily without the help of animals.

Weeds are part of a group known as pioneer plants. These plants are the first step in restoring the plant community after a disaster or after a harvest. They protect the newly exposed soil from erosion and help the ground to hold water and nutrients. Once the weeds have established, animals can feed and shelter. Animals bring in more seeds and larger plants grow.

In colder seasons, weeds provide habitat for pollinators when there is little else around. Climate change is affecting world temperatures and pollinators are appearing earlier in the year. Weeds are vital for these creatures to be able to exist in our changing world.

MARVELLOUS MOSS

Some plants are so commonly seen that you forget to notice them, and it is easy to assume that they don't do anything special. But, in the case of moss, you would be very wrong!

Mosses don't have roots. Instead, they have tiny hairlike structures, called rhizoids, that help them cling to surfaces. Rhizoids can help mosses to take in water, but some mosses can also absorb water through their surfaces.

Moss is a pioneer plant. It can grow on bare ground, even on rocks or roofs. It spreads by spores: tiny living cells that are released into the air by a parent plant. Mosses grow all over the world and can survive both extreme heat and cold. In fact, they are one of the only plants to live in the frozen continent of Antarctica.

In cold regions, moss protects the ground from melting; in hot regions, it protects tree roots from drying out. One type of moss has even adapted to growing in dark caves. These spooky plants seem to glow as they gather the little available light.

People have found some handy uses for moss too. In a process called phytofiltration, moss can be used to clean water that has been contaminated by the mining industry. It can also be used in swimming pool systems, removing the need for harsh chemicals, which is better for people and the environment.

ESSENTIAL POLLINATORS

A ripe red strawberry, a juicy yellow peach, a long green runner bean ... these treats and many more like them would disappear without the work of pollinators. Luckily, plants have the answers.

The plant-pollinator relationship is one of the best-known natural partnerships. Although you might immediately think of bees as pollinators, bats, birds, butterflies, moths and beetles all do the job too. Plants feed pollinators and provide their home and in return pollinators fertilise them.

Plants produce flowers with colours and scents to attract pollinators. When pollinators visit flowers, they feed on a sweet syrup called nectar. At the same time, a sticky dust called pollen attaches to their bodies. When the pollinator visits another plant, the pollen rubs off. This exchange of pollen fertilises the plant, allowing it to make seeds.

Producing seeds is a plant's way of surviving. By eating the seeds, fruits and vegetables that plants make, humans take in the proteins, vitamins, sugars and minerals we need to grow. We can plant the trees for fruit crops, but we will always rely on pollinators for the best crops of fruit.

Some plant seeds grow inside shells, such as nuts, or inside pods, such as peas. Others are hidden inside fruits and vegetables.

Pollinators face threats from human activity. To feed our vast populations, our farms are getting bigger. This clears wild land that pollinators live in. Many farms also use chemical pesticides that poison creatures that damage plants, but also the pollinators that feed on them.

PERFECT PARTNERS

The Joshua tree and the yucca moth have a unique pollination partnership. The tree doesn't make nectar to attract the moth, but the moth still comes to the tree. She lays her eggs in the flowers, pollinating them as she goes. The tree can then produce seeds, which are also food for young.

The yucca moth is the only insect that pollinates the Joshua tree, so the relationship is vital to its survival. The Joshua tree is essential to the desert ecosystem providing food and shelter for rodents and birds who, otherwise, would not be able to live there.

Baobab trees grow in Madagascar, mainland Africa and Australia. These 'tree of life' trees support both animal and human communities. Their enormous trunks store water for times of drought and elephants chew the bark when water is scarce.

Baobab flowers open at night, providing food for bats who pollinate them in return. Other animals make homes in the tree's hollows and branches. Its leaves and fruit are highly nutritious and can be eaten by both animals and humans. These trees provide shade and shelter from the heat, and older trees with hollow trunks can also provide useful storage or hiding places!

These plant-animal partnerships exist throughout nature, helping plants and animals survive difficult conditions. They have evolved over thousands of years of working together as a community.

SEED SURVIVAL

For plants to survive it is essential that they create their next generation. Plants have evolved incredible ways to keep their seeds safe and to make sure that they grow.

Once every few years, the dry brown earth of the Atacama Desert in Chile is flooded with colour. This region has almost no rainfall at all. There are even parts where rainfall has never been recorded. And yet, when rain does arrive, it is followed by a flower super bloom!

Where do the flowers come from? The answer is that their seeds were there all along, lying in wait for the rain. The water washes a protective coating off the seeds and they sprout. The harsh desert conditions mean the plants have adapted to grow and produce new seeds quickly.